SMYTHE GAMBRELL LIBRARY
WESTMINSTER ELEMENTARY SCHOOLS
1424 WEST PACES FERRY RD., N. W.
ATLANTA, GA. 30327

W9-ATB-712

WESTMINSTER SCHOOLS

SMYTHE
GAMBRELL
LIBRARY

PRESENTED BY

Mary Hurt and
Noble Stafford
1990

Will

The Seal Oil Lamp

THE SEAL OIL LAMP

Adapted from an Eskimo folktale and
illustrated with wood engravings by

DALE DE ARMOND

Sierra Club Books   **Little, Brown and Company**
San Francisco   Boston   Toronto

The Sierra Club, founded in 1892 by John Muir, has devoted itself to the study and protection of the earth's scenic and ecological resources—mountains, wetlands, woodlands, wild shores and rivers, deserts and plains. The publishing program of the Sierra Club offers books to the public as a nonprofit educational service in the hope that they may enlarge the public's understanding of the Club's basic concerns. The Sierra Club has some sixty chapters in the United States and in Canada. For information about how you may participate in its programs to preserve wilderness and the quality of life, please address inquiries to Sierra Club, 730 Polk Street, San Francisco, CA 94109.

A YOLLA BOLLY PRESS BOOK
Copyright © 1988 by Dale DeArmond

All rights reserved. No part of this book may be reproduced in any form or by any electronic or mechanical means, including information storage and retrieval systems, without permission in writing from the publisher, except by a reviewer who may quote brief passages in a review.

First Edition

Library of Congress Cataloging-in-Publication Data

DeArmond, Dale.
  The seal oil lamp / by Dale DeArmond.   1st ed.
    p. cm.
  Summary: A retelling of a traditional Eskimo tale of how a seven-year-old blind boy is saved from death by the kindly little mouse people.
  ISBN 0-316-17786-5 :
    1. Eskimos—Legends.   2. Indians of North America—Legends.
[1. Eskimos—Legends.   2. Indians of North America—Legends.]
I. Title.
E99.E7D346   1988
398.2' 08997—dc19   88–7272
                                            CIP
                                            AC

BP

10 9 8 7 6 5 4 3 2 1

Sierra Club Books/Little, Brown children's books are published by Little, Brown and Company (Inc.) in association with Sierra Club Books.

Printed in the United States of America

For Heather and Jamie

GLOSSARY

Allugua (Al-OO-gwa) A child's name.

Cache (cash) A food storage platform built on posts or poles, out of the reach of animals.

Inua (ee-NEW-ah) Soul or spirit. Each living thing, in the Eskimo belief, has an inua which can take other forms.

Oomiak (OO-mee-ack) A large skin boat used for hunting and for transportation.

Parka (PAR-kee) A hooded, coatlike, fur outer garment.

Shaman (SHAW-man) A medicine man or witch doctor, conjuror.

The Seal Oil Lamp

Come in, children. It's cold tonight but the old seal oil lamp will keep us warm, just like it did a long time ago when I was a girl and everyone sat around at night and told stories.

This story happened right here in our village way back when my grandma was a little girl. The village was different then. There wasn't any school. Nobody knew how to read or write. Mothers and fathers taught their children what they needed to know. Fathers taught their sons how to hunt birds and animals and how to build sleds and oomiaks, and all the other things men needed to know. They taught them to obey all the laws of the people and how to sing the songs and do the dances that honor the birds and the animals and please the inuas.

Mothers taught their daughters how to take care of the meat the hunters brought in and how to care for the skins of the animals and make them soft. They taught them to make clothes from the animal skins and to pull sinews from the legs of caribou to make sewing thread. Girls learned how to find greens and berries in the summer and put them away for the long winter, how to catch fish and dry them, and all the other things women needed to know. And girls, too, learned to obey the laws of the people.

In those days there wasn't any village store where you could buy flour and canned peaches and pretty flowered cloth for parka covers.

The houses people lived in were different then. They were very small and partly underground so they would keep warm just with the heat from the seal oil lamps. The roof was made from pieces of driftwood and whalebone and covered with sod. One layer of sod was laid over the driftwood and whalebone with the grass side down, and the next layer with the grass side up. When it was all finished it looked like a little mound with grass and flowers

growing on it in summer. In winter the snow covered it
and helped keep it warm. A hole was left in the roof to let
the smoke out, and there was a seal gut cover to put over
the hole when it was very cold or when snow was falling.

Inside the house there were no tables or chairs. Instead
there were benches along the walls where people slept or
sat. Sometimes they just sat on the floor. There were warm
furs on the benches for sleeping.

In most of the houses there were lots of children. But
in one house there was no child at all, and the man and
woman who lived in that house were very sad.

The man was a good hunter and captain of one of the big oomiaks that go out to look for the great whales when they pass in the spring. In winter he caught many seals, and when the walrus came by the village he was among the best of the walrus hunters too. He hunted caribou with the other men, and sometimes he hunted the great white bear.

He kept his wife supplied with skins and all the things she needed to make clothing for both of them. And, except in very bad years, there was always seal oil for the lamp and meat in the cache. He was a good man and kept all the laws of the people. He always thanked the animals for letting themselves be killed and was careful to return a part of each animal to the ocean so that the inuas could make more animals. He was generous with his neighbors and shared his kills with the old people who could no longer hunt, and with the widows who had no one to hunt for them and help them keep their children fed and clothed.

The woman was very good at preparing the skins of the animals and caring for the meat the men brought home. The clothing she made was beautiful and warm. She sewed the clothes with such tiny stitches that no cold or wet could get in. She knew where all the best greens grew, and where to find the finest berries. All summer long she gathered and stored food for the winter. No woman in the village could catch more fish or dry them more skillfully. She, too, obeyed the laws of the people and shared the good things with others who had less.

But these good people were sad because they had no children. All the other houses in the village were happy with the sounds of children laughing and playing. Only their house was still. The woman longed for a child to hold in her arms and carry in her parka hood like the other women. The man was sad, too, because there was no child to teach all the things he knew. But time went on and no child came. They asked the neighbors for advice, but the neighbors told them they could only wait and hope. They asked the shaman if he could help, and he danced his most powerful dance. When the dance was finished, he fell down exhausted and told them they could only wait and hope.

And so it was for a long time. Then one day the woman knew she was going to have a baby. She was so happy she sang all day long. The man was so happy that when he went hunting for seals his steps danced across the ice. As he went he sang softly to the seals:

> There will be a child in our house,
> Listen, seals.
> There will be a child in our house to laugh and play
> And I will teach him all the things he needs to know.
> Oh, I will teach him so many things.

When the child was born he was a beautiful little boy. They named him Allugua. He was a good and happy baby. But one day the father reached his hand toward the baby's face in play and the baby didn't even blink, though the father's hand was very near his eyes. The father tried again, then called his wife to bring something the baby liked, to see if he would reach for it. But the child just laughed and reached the other way and they knew their beautiful little boy was blind. The mother and father wept and they were afraid, for life was very hard in those days and it was the law of the people that no child could be allowed to live if he couldn't grow up to support himself. At last the mother said, "Maybe he wasn't quite

9

finished when he was born and his eyesight will come when he is a little older." So they comforted themselves, and the little boy was so merry and good and could do so many things, they almost forgot he was blind.

When Allugua was old enough to run around and play with the other children, he joined in all their games and he could do almost everything the other children could do. The other children loved him because he was funny and kind and could tell wonderful stories. He never teased the smaller children, and when they fell down and cried he helped them up and made them laugh. He even joined in the jumping game in the spring when the ice breaks up and the children jump from one ice floe to the next. Another child would hold his hand and they would run and jump together.

The mother and father watched their boy grow strong and waited for his eyes to see. The father taught Allugua

always to be kind to animals and birds. He explained that they are just like people and must be treated with respect and kindness because they do us great service when they let us kill them for food and clothing. When a whale or a walrus or a seal is killed, a part of it must be returned to the ocean. When you do that, it pays honor to the animals and makes sure that there will always be more.

The year Allugua was seven years old there was an especially hard winter. One freezing night a tired and cold little mouse crept into Allugua's sleeping place. He remembered what his father had taught him and he held the mouse carefully in his hand all night to keep it warm and so he would not roll on it and crush it. In the morning, although there was little food and everyone was hungry, Allugua gave the mouse a few bites of his breakfast.

By that time Allugua's parents had to admit to themselves that he was never going to be able to see. So they were not surprised, as the long winter neared its end, when some of the people of the village said to them, "When we go to spring fish camp you must harden your hearts and leave Allugua behind to die. You know he will never be able to support himself. A blind man can't hunt. When we go you must leave him in the house and block the entrance and the smoke hole. The spring nights are very cold and the cold is kind. Soon it will make him feel warm and he will fall asleep forever."

Both parents wept. The mother could not be comforted, but at last she told Allugua they must leave him to die because he could never get food for himself and would always be a burden on the village. Poor little Allugua was very sad and frightened, but he knew it was the law of the people and it must be.

When all the village people set off for the fish camp
Allugua's parents sadly told him good-bye. His mother held
him in her arms one last time and told him to be a brave
boy and to remember that the spirits are kind to little
children. They left him a little food and some water. The
mother secretly used the last bit of oil to light the seal oil
lamp so that Allugua would be warm for a little while.
And then they left him. Allugua heard the sounds they
made as they blocked the entrance to the house and the

smoke hole. He knew that his mother would leave a little opening so the smoke from the seal oil lamp could escape. At last they were done and he heard their departing footsteps creaking in the snow. Once the footsteps paused and Allugua thought they might change their minds and come back for him. Then the footsteps started again and grew fainter and fainter until at last he could hear only the lonely song of the wind.

Allugua cried for a little while, but he wasn't in the habit of feeling sorry for himself, so he sat up and sang all the songs he knew. Then he told himself all the stories he could remember. After a while he felt hungry, so he ate a little of the food his mother had left and drank some of the water. He curled himself up on the bedplace and went to sleep.

When Allugua woke in the morning the house was still warm, and when he went near the little lamp he found it was still burning. He was very surprised; his mother had left only a little oil in the lamp, so he thought he must have slept only a short time. He was very hungry, so he ate the few mouthfuls of food that were left and drank some water.

After he had eaten, Allugua played his game of sticks and stones, tossing a stone into the air, picking up the sticks with his other hand, and catching the stone before it reached the floor. Allugua was good at games like that, despite his blindness, because his hands were so quick and clever.

All that day he played his game and sang songs to himself and told himself stories. And all that day the little lamp continued to burn. It was still burning when he went to sleep that night.

When Allugua woke the next morning he was hungry and thirsty, but all the food and water were gone. He cried a little, but then he stopped for he thought he heard a very small sound coming from the passageway. He knew all the people had gone and he wondered what could be making the sound and he was a little afraid. Then a small, clear voice said, "Allugua, why were you crying?"

Allugua was surprised but he said, "I was crying because I'm all alone and hungry and thirsty and I'm afraid. All the people have gone to fish camp and left me here to die because I am blind and can't learn to hunt and get food."

"Ah, but you are not going to die, Allugua," said the small voice. "Put out your hand. There is food and clear, cold water by the seal oil lamp." Allugua put out his hand and it was true. There was food and water.

"Who are you?" he asked.

"Do you remember the little mouse who crept into your bed and you held it in your hand and kept it safe and warm? That little mouse was my child and I am Mouse Woman. Now my people will take care of you and keep you safe and warm.

"You are not going to die, Allugua. You are going to live and grow up to be a great man in your village."

Then the little Mouse Woman went away, but every day she returned with food and water, and the seal oil lamp continued to burn.

Summer is a busy time for the mouse people. They must fill their burrows with food to last all winter. But every day some of the mouse people came to see Allugua. They told him wonderful stories about the mouse world and about the owls and the foxes and the eagles who try to catch them, and how the mouse people outwit their enemies. They told him about Raven and the magic that lives under the earth and in the sky country. And the mouse people sang their songs for him and did their dances on the back of his hand so he could feel how beautiful their dances were.

One day Mouse Woman came to Allugua and said,
"I am going to teach you a magic hunting song. You must
always sing it very quietly to yourself so no one else can
hear it. But the animals will hear it and they will come to
you to be killed so you will always have food and clothing.
You must remember that this song is a gift from the animals and you must pay them honor and make songs and
dances for them. And you must always return a part of
each creature to the ocean so that the inuas can make
more animals."

Allugua promised to remember, so Mouse Woman
sang the magic hunting song in her small, clear voice.
She sang it over until Allugua could sing the song himself.
Then Mouse Woman left him alone in the little house.
This is the song:

> I am Allugua
> The blind one.
> Come to my knife and spear
> That I may live.
> I will make a song in your honor
> And all the people will know
> How strong and brave you were.

Spring and summer passed in a long dream of stories and songs and dances. In the fall, at the first frost, Mouse Woman came to Allugua early one morning and said, "Today the village people will return from fish camp. So we will leave you, but remember all we have taught you and don't tell anyone how we have helped you."

Allugua thanked Mouse Woman and promised to remember all the things that the mouse people had taught him. And he promised to keep the secret of the magic hunting song. Then he cried a little because he would miss Mouse Woman and her people.

When evening came he heard the voices of his own people. His heart beat fast because he knew his mother and father would soon enter the house and find him alive after such a long time. At last the mother crept into the house expecting to see her beloved son dead of cold and hunger. When she saw him sitting there strong and well she was so surprised and happy that she cried. And when the father came he also cried. Then they all went out to show the other people that Allugua was alive and well.

When his mother asked him how he stayed alive all that time he told her that the food and water she had left had lasted a long time. All the people agreed that it was wonderful that Allugua didn't die. They decided some magic had kept him alive and that he should live and grow up with his people in the village.

So Allugua was allowed to run and shout and play with the other children. Now he had even more wonderful stories. He told them all the stories he had learned from the mouse people. At night when the seal oil lamp was lit, even the grown people came to listen to Allugua.

He told them the famous tale of Small One, the mouse all the other mice laughed at because he never grew, and how he earned honor when he squeaked the alarm and saved the other seed gatherers from the wicked owl.

He told them new Raven tales: How Raven went out walking one day, admiring the fine world he had made, and came to a swampy place where some cotton grass was growing. He picked two heads of cotton and blew on them and they turned into the first mice. "Ah," said Raven, "what pretty little creatures you are. I want you to have lots of children and live under the earth in warm burrows. You will eat grass and seeds and harm no one." And so it is to this day.

When Allugua was almost a man he asked his father to let him join the whaling crew. His father said, "No, of course you can't join the whaling crew. You're blind and you would just get in the way of the whalers."

But Allugua said, "Father, let me come with you. I will kill a whale. I know that I will kill a whale."

At last the whalers said he could come with them, but he must be quiet and keep out of the way.

Allugua sat very still in the oomiak and was quiet for a long time. He sang the hunting song Mouse Woman had given him, but so quietly that no one could hear him. After

a while he asked to be put in the bow of the oomiak with the whaling harpoon in his hand. The men just laughed at him, but he insisted and kept saying, "Let me up there. I will kill a whale. I know I will kill a whale." At last the men got tired of listening to him and let him stand in the bow of the oomiak with the whaling harpoon in his hand. Suddenly a whale came very close and the men yelled, "Dart him! Dart him!"

But Allugua said, "No, that isn't the right one," and went on singing his hunting song to himself.

Then the ice began to crowd in and the men quickly hauled the big oomiak to safety on the solid ice. Allugua went to the very edge of the ice, listening and singing his song. His ears were so very sharp from listening to the mouse people that he could hear the whales singing. He said, "I can hear them." But the men said, "He just hears the ice crowding."

Again a whale came close and again the men yelled, "Dart him! Dart him!" But again Allugua said, "No, that's not the right one."

Then Allugua beckoned the men to come forward. They did so, although they still believed that he was just hearing the crowding of the ice. Suddenly a great whale breached and Allugua threw the harpoon. The whale and harpoon went under the water, and the harpoon line was drawn out very fast. All the men rushed to help bring in the great whale Allugua had darted.

When the people saw the whalers returning towing the great whale, they rushed down to the shore shouting and laughing with joy. Many hands helped beach the whaling boat, and then everyone took hold of the tow lines and hauled the enormous whale high on the shore ice. All the while the whalers were shouting, "It's Allugua's whale! Allugua darted it himself." They told the wonderful story of the hunt over and over. It was a proud day for Allugua and his parents.

The men set to work at once cutting up the whale and dividing it among all the villagers, for everyone shared in the whale. At last there was nothing left but the great bones. Then what a feast they had! After the feast Allugua made a dance about the whale hunt and as he danced he sang a song to honor the whale, just as he had promised.

> Oh brave one,
> Oh strong one,
> How beautiful you were in the water.
> You came to my spear,
> You gave yourself to my spear.
> I mourn your proud death
> And I pay you honor and thanks this night.

Before the whaling season came to an end that year Allugua killed three more whales. The following year he did the same thing. Instead of being a poor blind man who was a burden to the village, Allugua became one of the greatest whalers the village ever had.

By and by he married a beautiful girl from the next village and they had many children. Allugua lived to be very old.

But for as long as he lived, Allugua remembered his promise to the Mouse Woman. He kept the secret of the magic hunting song, and he paid honor to the animals. He killed many whales, but he returned a part of each one to the ocean so there would always be more whales.

The text for this book was set by hand in Pegasus,
a typeface designed by Berthold Wolpe c. 1937
to complement Albertus, a display type also used here.
The book was designed and edited by James and
Carolyn Robertson at The Yolla Bolly Press,
Covelo, California. The type was set by Joel Benson,
Linda Gustafson, and Diana Fairbanks, who also
prepared pages for publication.